FARM
HOUSE

MOUNTAINS
THAT
WAY

TRUCK

GARDEN

WOODPILE

RED BARN

FENCE

A House For a Mouse

Written and Illustrated

by

Smith Roberts

Prospero's Press

BOULDER

Requests for permission to make copies
of any part of the work should be mailed to:
Permissions Department,
Prospero's Press, P.O. Box 4616
Boulder, CO 80306-4616.

Library of Congress Control Number: 2002096215

Roberts, Smith 1976–
A House for a Mouse/by Smith Roberts

Summary: When a young mouse named Jack
leaves home, he is faced with unexpected dangers
until he uses his wits to create a rather surprising
new house for himself.

ISBN 0-9727315-3-9

1.Mice– Juvenile Fiction
2. Halloween – Juvenile fiction.
[1. Mice– Fiction. 2. Halloween– Fiction.] I. Title

Printed in Singapore

For my parents

Once upon a time, there was a little mouse named Jack. The time had come for Jack to leave his parents' house and find a home of his own, as all young mice do.

First, Jack climbed a great big tree. He found a cozy hollow in the trunk of the tree, and he moved in.

"Ah," said Jack. "This is a good home for me."

The mean blue jay didn't think so, though.
"Only birds can live in trees!" said the blue jay. "Get out of here, mouse!"

And with a mean squawk, the blue jay chased Jack away.

So with a sigh, Jack set out to find a new home.

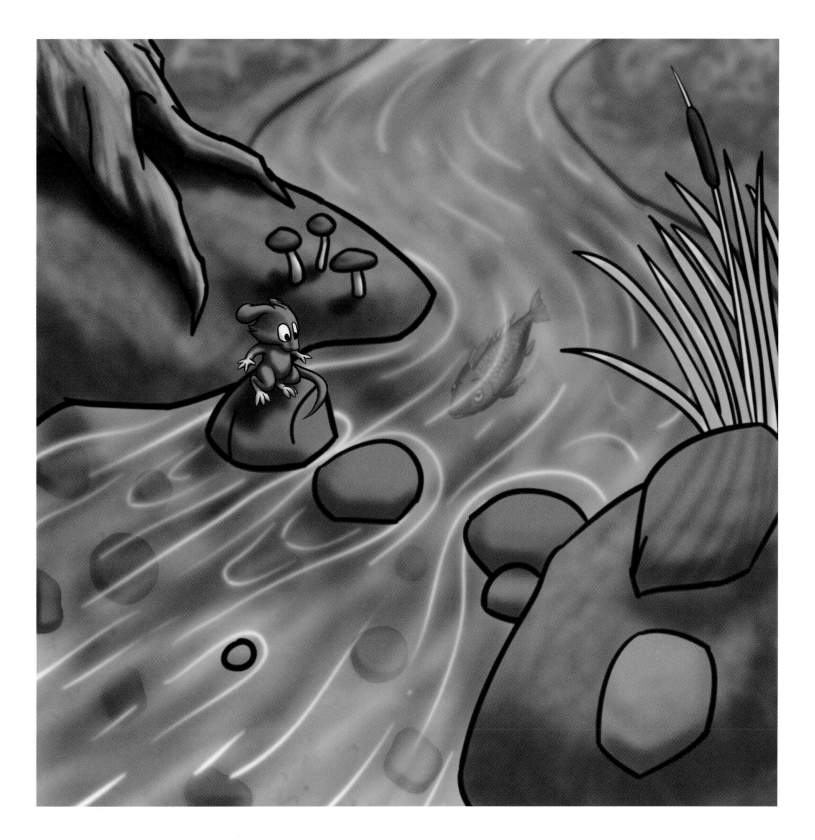

Next, Jack dug a hole deep in to the side of a hill. Soon he had built a comfortable burrow in the ground, and he moved in.

"Ah," said Jack. "This is a nice home for me."

But the mean snake didn't think so.

"Thisss hole fitsss me nicely," said the snake. "Sssscram, moussse!"

And with a mean hiss, the snake chased Jack away.

So with a sigh, Jack set out to find a new home.

Next, Jack explored the big woodpile by the barn. He found a dry space between the logs, and he moved in. "Ah," said Jack. "This is a great home for me."

However, the mean weasel didn't think so.

"This is my woodpile," said the weasel. "Go away mouse, or I will eat you for lunch!"

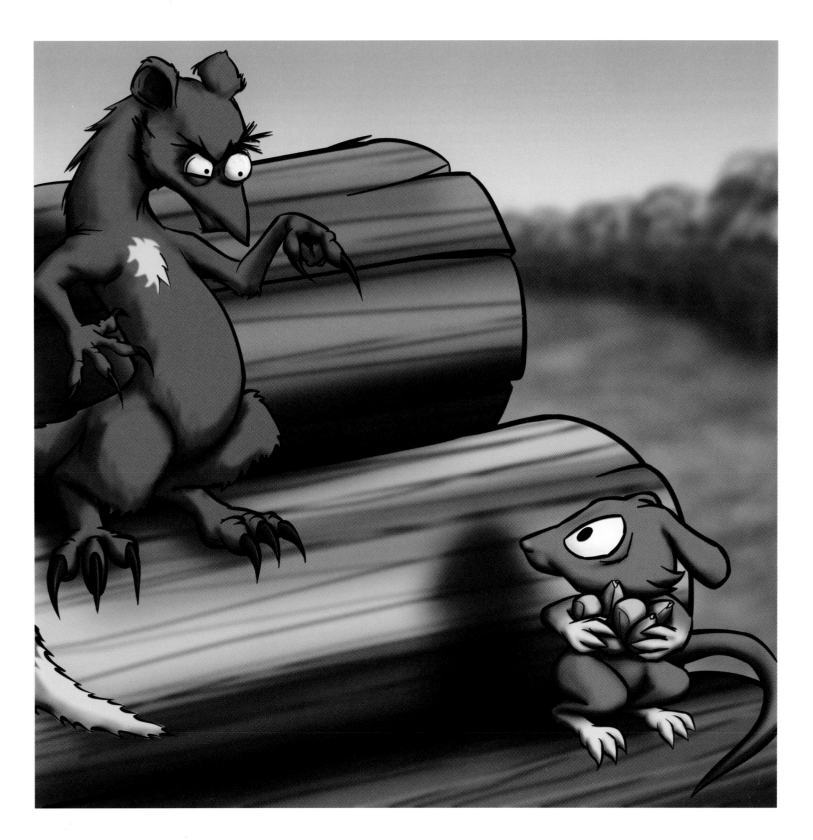

And with a mean chattering, the weasel chased Jack away.

So with a sigh, Jack set out to find a new home.

Next, Jack found a secret way into the farmhouse. There he made a nice hole for himself inside the wall.

"Ah," said Jack. "This is a wonderful home for me."

Except the mean rat didn't think so.

"I'm moving in!" said the rat. "Get out of my way, mouse!"

And with a mean squeak, the rat chased Jack away.

Jack was very sad. But he didn't give up.
"I'll show those big, mean animals!" said Jack.
So once again Jack set out to find a new home.

Jack found a big orange pumpkin at the edge of the garden. He looked it up and down, then started turning it into a house.

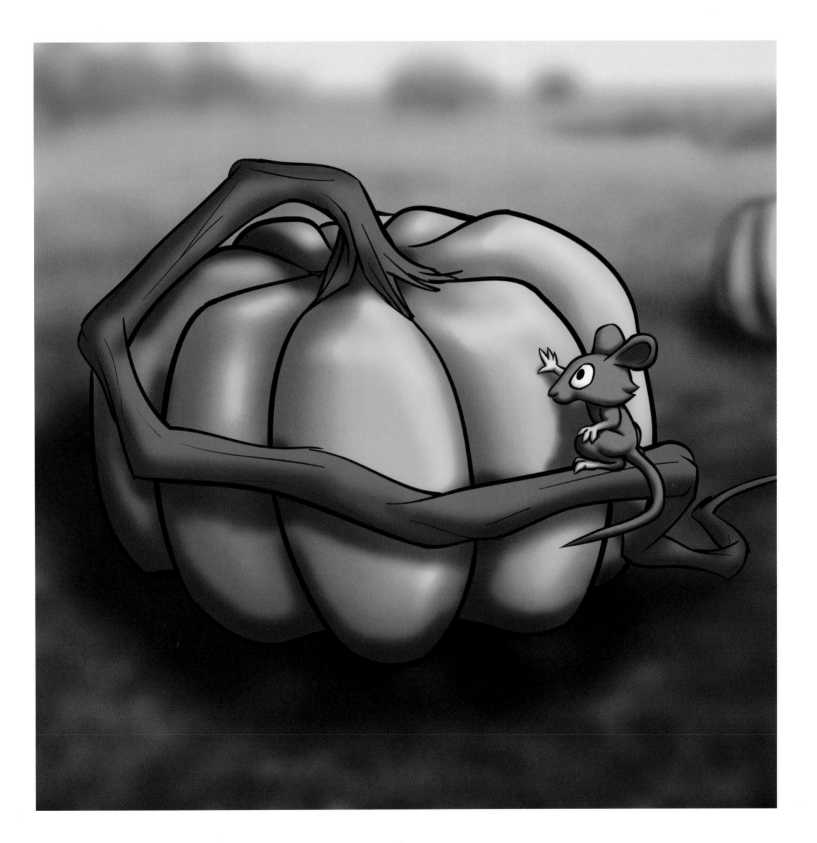

Jack cut a hole in the pumpkin to use as his door. He didn't want any big animals to get in, so he made it only big enough for a mouse.

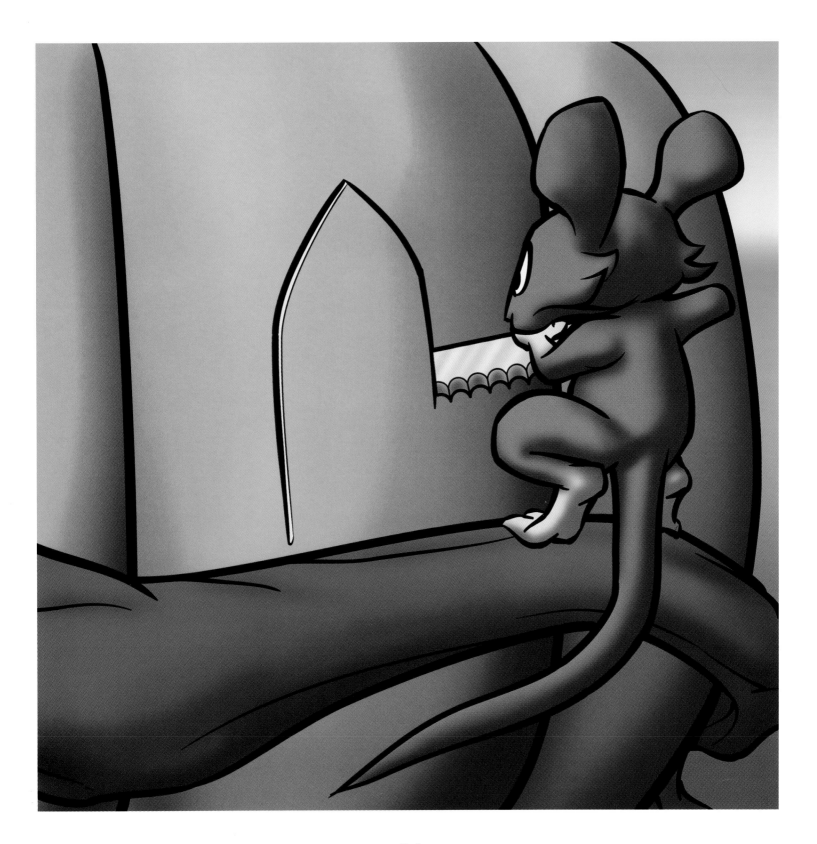

After he had cleaned out the insides of the pumpkin, Jack decided he needed windows. It was too dark in there! So he cut two more holes up high where the sun could shine in.

But with all these small doors and windows, Jack couldn't fit his bed inside!

So he cut one last hole, just barely big enough to slide his bed through.

That night, Jack left his candle burning as he went to bed.

"This is a perfect home for me," he whispered. "I hope none of the other animals take it from me!"

But, of course, all the other animals were far too afraid of Jack's new home even to go near it.

The End